'You knock now,' Mr Wheel
'Don't be scared. Knock on
as you like.'

At first Michaela didn't want to. Then she thought it
was too good a chance to miss. She went closer to the
table and knocked twice quickly – then added
another knock after a pause.

From the stair door behind her came two quick
knocks, then a pause, and then a third knock.
Michaela spun round and stared at the door.

'It's very strange,' Mrs Lloyd said, drawing out a
chair and sitting down.

''Tain't strange at all,' Mr Wheeler said. 'It's our
Jack! I've lived with him all my life, growed up with
him. I *know* he's real . . . '

When eight-year-old Michaela and her mum move
into Mr Wheeler's wonderful old house, he warns
them that the house is haunted – by a noisy ghost
named Jack. Michaela thinks that living with Jack
could be fun, even if they do have to follow funny
rules to keep the ghost happy. But does he really
exist? Michaela is determined to find out!

ABOUT THE AUTHOR

SUSAN PRICE has worked as a lecturer, a dishwasher, a museum guide, a supermarket assistant and general assistant in a warehouse. She is the author of more than twenty titles for children, the majority involving ghosts in one form or another. In 1987, she was awarded the Carnegie Medal for her book *Ghost Drum*, an award for which a previous title *Odin's Monster* was also nominated. She has also won the Other Award with *Twopence a Tub*. *Knocking Jack* is her first book to be published by Yearling. She lives in the West Midlands.

KNOCKING JACK

SUSAN PRICE

ILLUSTRATED BY JON RILEY

YEARLING BOOKS

KNOCKING JACK
A YEARLING BOOK 0 440 862817

First publication in Great Britain

PRINTING HISTORY
Yearling edition published 1992

Conditions of sale

This book is set in 14/16pt Century Schoolbook by
Chippendale Type Ltd., Otley, West Yorkshire.

Yearling Books are published by Transworld Publishers Ltd.,
61–63 Uxbridge Road, Ealing, London W5 5SA, in Australia by
Transworld Publishers (Australia) Pty. Ltd., 15–23 Helles
Avenue, Moorebank, NSW 2170, and in New Zealand by
Transworld Publishers (N.Z.) Ltd., Cnr. Moselle and
Waipareira Avenues, Henderson, Auckland.

Made and printed in Great Britain by
Guernsey Press Ltd., Guernsey, Channel Islands

CHAPTER ONE

'Where are we going, anyway?' Michaela asked.

'Wait until we get there and see.'

'But I might not want to go. If you tell me where we're going, I can decide whether I want to go or not.'

'You'll want to go,' her mother said. 'Besides, I can't go without you. I need your advice.'

'No, you don't,' Michaela said. She knew when people were trying to flatter her into doing something.

'Yes, I do. I can't make up my mind about this without you being there.'

'Tell me!' Michaela said.

'No. Come along and see.'

Michaela could see that she was going to have to go, and put up with being bored if the destination turned out to be somewhere dull. From the table she picked up the little red box her grandfather had given her just a few days before, having found it in the back of a cupboard in the shed. The box was small and oval-shaped, with a lid that pulled off and fitted on again so tightly that you could hardly see where the box ended and

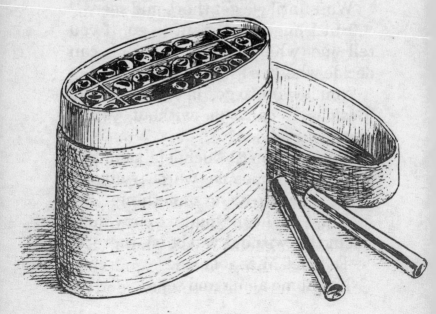

the lid began. It was made of the thinnest wood, covered with something that her grandfather called 'flock'. It was like thin red paper, but it felt like velvet when she rubbed her thumb over it. When she pulled the lid off and put her nose inside it, she could smell wood.

Inside, the box was divided into little compartments with thin, thin slices of wood, all fitted together. The compartments held little silver pipes. They were smooth and round, fat and heavy, and cold to touch; and they all smelled of metal. The round holes at one end were partly blocked off with a half-circle of metal, and on this half-circle was engraved the name of the pipe: 'A' or 'C', or 'G'. When you put a pipe in your mouth and blew, they each played a different note. Her grandfather said they were tuning-pipes, to help in tuning a piano. Michaela loved them. She loved everything about them: their box and its compartments, and its furry red cover and its smell. The pipes and their roundness, their coolness and heaviness and their beautiful sounds. She even liked the way they rattled and chinked in their box as she carried them out to the car.

She climbed into the passenger seat when her mother opened the door, and fastened her seat-belt. 'I bet this is going to be boring,' she said.

'You think everything's going to be boring, Misery.'

Michaela had opened her box, and she took out the pipe with the deepest and most mournful sound. She blew it. Her mother sighed.

The drive was quite long, but once they were through the town they were able to join the big main road and tear along at forty miles an hour. Michaela watched the speedometer and blew a high-pitched note whenever they went too fast. They passed the secondary school where her mother taught English and History and, a few moments later, they turned uphill at another set of traffic lights. The hill was steep, and Michaela looked expectantly at the gear-stick, smiling when she saw her mother reach out and change down into third. They turned right again at a big public house and started driving up another, even steeper hill. On one side of them were houses, on the other side, tall hedges. An occasional gap in the hedge let them see the golf course on the other side of it. Halfway up this steep hill, her mother swung the car right again, off the road and into a drive. 'Here we are,' she said, and turned and looked at Michaela.

Michaela peered through the windscreen at the house they had stopped outside. It was an old house. You could tell that by the thick grey wooden beams that criss-crossed the red brick, and by the way the roof sagged and bumped. It was a long house, and the door was nearer to one end than the other. The door was big

and made of polished wooden planks. There were two big windows as well, windows taller than the door, with pointed tops, like church windows. The house had two chimneys, one at either end. A plant – a clematis her mother said – grew up the wall and over part of the roof, and was covered with flowers that looked like little yellow lanterns.

'Have we come to visit it?' Michaela asked. Her mother sometimes took her and her friends to see ruined castles or old houses. The castles were fun, but the houses, where you had to walk round behind a guide and listen to a lot of talk — they were boring.

'Yes, we've come to visit it,' said her mother, but in an excited sort of way that made Michaela think she meant more than she said.

Michaela climbed out of her side of the car and waited while her mother locked up. She sorted through her box of pipes, blowing them experimentally until she found the one that she thought suited the house best. She blew the pipe gently, making a low, long-drawn-out note of curiosity.

The big wooden door of the house opened and a tall old man came out, leaning on a walking-stick. He stopped a pace or two from the house, and her mother hurried over to him. 'Mrs Lloyd?' he asked, holding out his hand.

'Mr Wheeler? Yes, I'm Mrs Lloyd — pleased to meet you. This is my daughter, Michaela. Michaela, say hello to Mr Wheeler.'

'Hello,' Michaela said, hanging back and feeling suspicious of Mr Wheeler. She didn't know why he was meeting them at the door.

'Come in, come in,' Mr Wheeler said, pointing at the open door with his stick. 'After you, ladies. Go straight down the passage and into the first door on your left.'

Mrs Lloyd pushed Michaela ahead of her into the house, so Michaela found herself leading the way down a long, narrow and rather dark passage that smelt of wood and polish and also – faintly – of coffee. Behind her she could hear the quick footsteps of her mother, and the shuffling of the old man, echoing between the wooden walls. There was another sound too: it sounded like someone knocking on a wooden door. But if someone was knocking on the door, it had nothing to do with her, and she said to herself, 'I write with my left hand, so the door will be on the side I write with.' By holding out her left hand, she found the door and turned through it.

She went into a big kitchen. It was half what she expected, and half not. There were the big, uneven red tiles on the floor, and the huge fireplace, like those she'd seen in other historical houses her mother had taken her to. There was a big wooden table in the middle of the room, with chairs round it, and a big and old-looking Welsh dresser with crockery stacked on it. But the room was painted yellow and white, and there was a modern sink and gas stove and some modern cupboards too. She went over to the fireplace, walked into it, and stood looking up into the cold darkness of the chimney.

Mr Wheeler and her mother came in behind her. 'I thought you'd like some tea afore you looked the house over,' the old man was saying. 'Would you like to serve, Mrs Lloyd? There's some squash for the little wench if her don't like tea.'

He lowered himself carefully on to a chair, and watched as Mrs Lloyd began serving tea. 'Michaela, come and have some pop and biscuits.'

Michaela came slowly over to the table and climbed on to a chair. There were biscuits, jammy-dodgers, arranged on a plate in the middle of the table. Her mother gave her two with her glass of squash. Michaela crunched one of them and looked at Mr Wheeler from the corners of her eyes. He had a grey moustache, and a lot of hair for an old man. Something strange was going on, she thought. When you visited a house like this, you usually paid money at the door, and there were usually a lot of people. You weren't taken into the kitchen and given biscuits.

'We've lived here time out of mind,' Mr Wheeler said. 'For years I've been saying I wouldn't leave, but I can't manage these stairs no more, nor

these floors, all uneven. I come a
right tumble down them stairs—' He
pointed with his stick to a door in the
far corner of the kitchen. The door
didn't look like stairs to Michaela.

'Folk would have paid to see it,' Mr Wheeler was going on. 'It's lucky our Julie found me afore I'd been lying there long. And now I've been moved in with her. I said, why don't you move in here, but her won't have that. No central heating, no washing machines. I said, there's more to house than central heating, but it's no use talking. Her rules me. I had to move into her place, and leave this standing empty . . . I've got steel pins in me leg,' he said unexpectedly to Michaela. 'Big steel pins like safety-pins to hold me together, 'cos I'm falling apart. But you two'll have no trouble with the stairs. You'll fly up 'em like you had wings.'

While he'd been talking, someone had knocked on the door again. Michaela knew that her mother heard it by the way she looked towards the sound, but Mr Wheeler didn't seem to notice. 'Is someone at the door?' Mrs Lloyd asked.

'No, no,' Mr Wheeler said, and

added something else about his daughter, Julie.

Michaela slid off her chair and went over to the door in the corner. She opened it and found, behind it, a steep flight of stairs that turned a corner and disappeared in darkness. Behind her, her mother and Mr Wheeler were pushing their chairs back and getting up. Mr Wheeler led the way out of the kitchen into the dark passage. Michaela shut the door and hurried after them.

Mr Wheeler led them through a door opposite the kitchen, into a large, high room. Michaela had to tip her head right back to see the ceiling – it was twice as high as in the kitchen. High up there were arching wooden beams, interlocking across the width of the room – the kind of beams that she'd only seen before in castles.

'This is the hall,' Mr Wheeler said. It didn't look like a hall to Michaela. To her, a hall was a long, narrow

corridor leading from the front door to the other rooms. She brought her gaze down from the ceiling to the floor. This hall was a huge room. The sitting-room and front-room of her gran's house would have fitted into it. The expanse of wooden floor was hardly covered by a couple of old rugs, and the only furniture – a sofa, a low table, a couple of mismatched arm-chairs and an old sideboard – looked tiny and lost, awash in the bright light that came in through the tall windows on either side of the room. The light from the two windows met in the middle of the room and seemed to melt everything away.

Michaela went over to one of the windows. Their deep sills had been turned into seats. She sat down on one, grinning with delight at its oddity. Looking up, she saw Mr Wheeler grinning back at her, show-ing big yellow teeth under his grey moustache, as if he was pleased that she was pleased. 'It's nice to sit there in summer,' he said. 'Bloody cold in the winter— Oh, excuse me, Mrs Lloyd. But it's a difficult room to heat.'

'I can imagine,' Mrs Lloyd said. 'There's no fireplace.'

'Well, the fire used to be in the middle, days gone by.'

'It's incredible that a house so old has been so little altered,' Mrs Lloyd said.

'Well,' said Mr Wheeler, 'it'd be unlucky to alter it much.' He pointed across the hall with his stick to another door. 'That's the parlour through there. That's a warm room for the winter.' He led the way across the hall, leaning on his stick, moving awkwardly. He glanced back at Michaela. 'You stay there if you want to.'

But Michaela jumped off the windowseat as soon as they had gone through the door into the parlour. She was too curious to be left behind.

The parlour was much smaller and lower than the hall, but it was still a large room. From the moment they entered, a noise started. It was like someone knocking on wood, but quickly and continually. At times, it almost sounded like a drum solo. They stood looking at the beautiful window with its pointed arches – like the ones in the hall only smaller – and admiring the tiny pink flowers on the white wallpaper, and the deep pink carpet, and all the time the knocking went on. Going close to her mother, Michaela whispered, 'What's that noise?'

'Ssh,' Mrs Lloyd whispered back. 'It's probably water in the pipes – old pipes.'

That reminded Michaela of her pipes and she felt in her pocket for them. They weren't there. She was looking round for where she'd left them when she saw that the parlour window had a seat built into it as well, and she forgot about her pipes as she ran across to claim the seat by sitting on it.

'Television,' Mr Wheeler said, pointing it out with his stick. 'You can build a lovely fire in that grate. This was my wife's favourite room when she was alive.'

'It is a lovely room,' Mrs Lloyd said with a big smile.

Mr Wheeler showed his large teeth in an answering smile, and pointed with his stick to a door at the back of the room. 'You go and have a look upstairs by yourself. I'll stop down here.'

Mrs Lloyd smiled and started up the stairs. Michaela began to follow but, as she passed Mr Wheeler, the old man touched her shoulder and said, 'When you go upstairs, look at the wall on your right as you go in and you'll see a little door. You go up and open that.'

Behind the door Mrs Lloyd had left open there was another steep, cramped flight of stairs. They were so steep that Michaela found it easier to go up them on all fours than to climb upright. At the top was a single door, and that opened into a room nearly as big as the parlour beneath. The floor sloped away from her, made of dark, twisted planks of wood. Light poured across the room from the one small window which, sadly, had no windowseat. There were two single beds with a chest standing between them, with a lamp on it; and there was also a wardrobe and a dressing-table with a mirror. All the furniture was old-fashioned. Michaela looked round for the little door Mr Wheeler had mentioned.

There it was in the wall, a little square door with a little iron latch holding it closed. She reached up, lifted the latch, and the door swung open, but although she could reach the latch, the door was too high for her to see through. What was it? A cupboard? What was in it? She called her mother and Mrs Lloyd came across.

'Peculiar,' she said, looked through the door, and then laughed.

'What is it?' Michaela demanded. 'I can't see.'

Mrs Lloyd looked round to see if there was something for Michaela to stand on and, seeing nothing, took hold of her daughter round the waist to lift her up. 'Come on then, you big lump. Heave!'

Michaela was hoisted into the air and grasped the edges of the little door. In a giddying way, she found herself looking down into the hall they'd just left. And there was Mr Wheeler, seen from an odd angle, leaning on his stick and grinning and waving.

With a gasp, Mrs Lloyd dropped her daughter back to the wooden floor. 'I could see Mr Wheeler!' Michaela said. 'Downstairs! It's a peephole!'

'Yes.' Mrs Lloyd stood looking around the room thoughtfully. 'This was probably the solar,' she said. 'That's a private room for the family that owned the house. It's an old place, this; it's what's called a hall house. The hall down there – that's where everyone used to live, all together. The family that owned the house, their servants, everyone. They might even have kept animals in part of it.'

'Dogs?' Michaela said, thinking that wasn't so unusual.

'No. Cows, sheep, pigs.'

'Urgh!'

'The private rooms were usually upstairs ... the room Mr Wheeler calls the parlour might have been a storeroom once – or animal stalls. This little peephole would have been for the master or mistress of the house to look down into the hall and see that everyone was behaving themselves.'

'Spying!' Michaela said. 'Lift me up again!'

'Oh no,' her mother said. 'You're getting too big for me, and besides, Mr Wheeler's waiting.' She led the way across to the stairs again.

'Is there more to see?' Michaela asked. When her mother nodded, she ran after her. Just as she was going through the door on to the stairs there was a noise behind her, as if something fairly small but hard – like a cricket ball – had been dropped on to the wooden floor. She looked back, but there was nothing that could have made the noise. And then she forgot it and hurried down the stairs. She was beginning to enjoy looking over this house. It was much better when you were the only people being shown around.

Mr Wheeler was sitting in one of the windowseats in the hall because he found them easier to get up from than an armchair. 'You like my little door?' he asked Michaela. She was shy of answering, but smiled to show that she did. 'Come and see t'other bedroom,' Mr Wheeler said to her mother.

He led them from the hall and across the passage into the kitchen. There he leaned against the dresser and left them to climb the steep stairs in the corner. At the top they came out into another bedroom, much smaller than the one with the spy-hole. There was a big old double bed, a small chest of drawers, and a strip of carpet.

'But there's a fireplace, look,' Mrs Lloyd said. 'All my life I've wanted to sleep in a bedroom with a fireplace.'

Michaela went to look out of the window. There were yellow lantern flowers right outside; and then she could see a red bus going past on the road below, and some people walking over the golf course on the other side of the road, dragging bags of clubs behind them. She turned round when her mother made a surprised sound.

Mrs Lloyd was looking round a door at the back of the room. 'The bathroom!' she said. 'I was wondering where it was.'

They went in. It wasn't the best bathroom Michaela had ever seen. It opened right off the bedroom, which she had never known a bathroom to do before. And then, it was very ugly. One of her friends had a bathroom where everything was pink, even the carpet and the toilet. The toilet-paper, the soap and the shampoo were pink as well, to match. This bathroom had a big, gaunt bath in harsh white enamel, and the enamel inside was stained. The basin and the lavatory were the same harsh white, and the taps were big, ugly and chrome. The floor was sloping and uneven like the other bedroom floor, and it was covered with crumbling, grubby old lino, instead of carpet.

'We've seen it all now,' Mrs Lloyd said, and started back downstairs.

Michaela followed her mother, feeling rather puzzled. This was an old house, but where were the furry, twisted ropes with brass hooks on the end, roping you off from the things you wanted to look at? Where were the big paintings on the walls and the suits of armour? And Mr Wheeler, who was supposed to be showing them round, had told them hardly anything about the house. Her mother had told her more. It wasn't at all like other visits she'd made to 'historical houses'.

'Excuse me for not getting up, Mrs Lloyd,' Mr Wheeler said, when they emerged from the stairway into the kitchen again. 'Come and have another cup of tea. It's still hot.'

'Is that someone at the door?' Mrs Lloyd asked. It sounded as if someone was knocking again – at the back door rather than the front one.

'Take no notice,' Mr Wheeler said. 'If you're going to live here, you'll have to get used to a bit of knocking.'

'Live here?' Michaela said, and stared at her mother.

Her mother smiled and looked rather embarrassed. 'Mr Wheeler's offering us the chance to rent the house from him.'

'I need somebody to look after it until me grandson comes back from America and takes it over,' the old man said. 'That won't be for five years or so.'

'Would you like to live here, Mikki?' her mother asked.

Michaela thought of the window-seats and the spy-hole and thought that yes, she *would* like to live here. 'But where are you going to live?' she said to Mr Wheeler.

'With me daughter. I've got me orders.'

'You've heard me mention my friend, Julie, from work?' Mrs Lloyd said. 'She's Mr Wheeler's daughter. She asked me if I'd like to rent the house in the first place.'

'We'll leave Gran and Grandad and come and live here?' Michaela asked, to make sure she had it right. Her mother nodded. 'Can Tiglet come as well?'

Mrs Lloyd looked at Mr Wheeler. 'Tiglet is Mikki's cat, Mr Wheeler. You don't mind pets, do you?'

'No!' the old man said. 'Pets, children, they're all welcome in this house. It's seen a good many of 'em!'

'If Tiglet can come, and Gran and Grandad can visit us, I'd like to live here,' Michaela said.

Mrs Lloyd turned to the old man with a smile and said, 'Then it's settled, Mr Wheeler!'

Mr Wheeler shifted on his chair and looked about in a vague, rather uncomfortable manner. 'Ah,' he said. 'Not yet. There's something I ain't told you yet.'

'What's that?'

'I don't know if I should say it in front of the little wench.'

'Mr Wheeler?' Mrs Lloyd said, completely puzzled.

'Well . . . Mrs Lloyd . . . Let me ask you . . . Do you believe in ghosts?'

Mrs Lloyd laughed. 'Not since I was Mikki's age!'

'That's difficult,' Mr Wheeler said. 'You see, this house is haunted.'

CHAPTER TWO

Michaela felt a shock of fear run through her and wasn't sure if she was excited and pleased, or simply scared. She stared at Mr Wheeler, who nodded back at her solemnly.

'Mr Wheeler, I wish you hadn't said that in front of Mikki now. She's only eight. Children do have nightmares.'

'Oh, this ain't a ghost to have nightmares about,' Mr Wheeler said. He looked up as there was another sound of knocking. This time it sounded as if someone was knocking on the floorboards in the small bedroom above their heads. 'That's him,'

Mr Wheeler said. 'That's our Jack. We've called him Knocking Jack in the family since – oh, time out of mind. You know, Mrs Lloyd, living here on your own, you'll never have to worry about burglars, not with Jack.'

'Oh – *Jack* will protect us from burglars,' Mrs Lloyd said. Michaela could see that she didn't believe a word of what Mr Wheeler was telling her, and was laughing at him. 'That'll save the expense of a dog.'

'Nobody who broke in here would stop long – but we never have been broke into that I know of. Jack's the good luck of the house, that's what my dad used to say donkey's years ago. The good luck of the house. But there's rules.'

'Terms and conditions. Of course,' Mrs Lloyd said.

'Not them kind of rules. All that's easy settled. I don't want you making any alteration to the fabric of the house, but apart from that, you must treat it as your own. No, I meant rules for when you're dealing with Jack.'

'Oh. *Jack's* rules,' Mrs Lloyd said, still in that half-laughing way.

'You don't believe me, do you, Mrs Lloyd?' Mr Wheeler said and, before she could answer, he called out, 'Jack!' and banged twice on the table.

From the room above came two answering knocks.

Mr Wheeler knocked five times on the table.

From the passage beside the kitchen, making Mrs Lloyd and Michaela jump, came five answering knocks.

'You knock now,' Mr Wheeler said to Michaela. 'Don't be scared. Knock on the table. As many times as you like.'

At first Michaela didn't want to. Then she thought it was too good a chance to miss. She went closer to the

table and knocked twice quickly —
then added another knock after a
pause.

From the stair door behind her
came two quick knocks, then a pause,

and then a third knock. Michaela spun round and stared at the door.

'You can keep it up all day, if you want,' Mr Wheeler said. Michaela looked at her mother's face and saw that it was shocked and pale. 'Noises in the pipes don't answer you, do they?' Mr Wheeler asked, and he rapped briskly three times on the table. From the kitchen door came three brisk knocks.

'It's – very strange,' Mrs Lloyd said, drawing out a chair and sitting down.

''Tain't strange at all,' Mr Wheeler said. 'It's our Jack! I've lived with him all my life, growed up with him. I *know* he's real, but I'm used to other folk not believing. Do you like washing-up, Mrs Lloyd?'

'No! Does anyone?'

'Well, Jack must. Keep the rules, Mrs Lloyd, and you need never do a day's washing-up while you live here. Nor tidying up, neither.'

'The ghost does the washing-up?'

Mrs Lloyd asked. 'I must say, that's the handiest ghost I ever heard of. I always thought ghosts just moaned and rattled chains.'

'Jack ain't that kind of ghost. I'll tell you what you must do. You must get to bed early if you don't want to be plagued. Jack likes the house to himself after about ten o'clock. And afore you go up you must leave Jack his dinner – like leaving mincepies and wine for Father Christmas,' the old man said to Michaela.

'Does Jack eat his dinner?' Mrs Lloyd asked. 'Whenever Michaela left anything for Father Christmas, he always left it for me.'

'Jack eats his dinner,' Mr Wheeler said, very seriously. 'The old 'uns used to say that he took the goodness out of it and left the food, and nobody should eat what he leaves 'cos it's got no goodness in it at all. I don't know about that, but I do know Jack misses his dinner if you don't leave it out. You must leave out his dinner, and you must not do any tidying up or washing-up yourself. Jack does it in the night.' Mrs Lloyd laughed. 'I'm telling you what you must do,' Mr Wheeler said, with a touch of annoyance, and Mrs Lloyd made herself serious again. Michaela was listening very solemnly. 'If you tidy up, Jack'll mess the place up in the night, and he can do a good job of that, believe me.'

'So I get to leave all the housework?' Mrs Lloyd said. 'Mr Wheeler, you could charge much more than you're asking for this place!'

'I know I could, but I want people I like and trust in it. I was also going to tell you that you must never, never forget to leave Jack's dinner or he'll pay you back for it.'

'How will he pay you back?' Michaela asked, fearfully.

'Oh, noise, mess. Treat him right and he'll treat you right, guard the house and bring good luck. But treat him wrong and you'll be sorry.'

'Mr Wheeler,' Mrs Lloyd said, frowning and nodding towards Michaela. She didn't want these odd stories to frighten her daughter.

'Porridge he likes,' Mr Wheeler said. 'And toast, 'specially with jam or honey. Stew, that'll do him. Bread and cheese. And a glass of milk. We always give him a treat if we was having owt special: a glass of beer or summat stronger at Christmas, chocolate at Easter. And we've been very happy here, my family. And will be, when my grandson comes back.'

'This is—?' Mrs Lloyd began. 'Excuse me, Mr Wheeler, but you're serious? This is really a condition of renting the house, that we put out meals for the ghost?'

'Yes,' Mr Wheeler said decidedly. 'Every night, without fail.'

Mrs Lloyd couldn't help laughing again. 'Sort of a peppercorn rent? I suppose it's little enough to ask. All right, Mr Wheeler, if it makes you happy.'

'It'll make *you* happy,' he said.

Mrs Lloyd then asked about rent books, and who would pay for repairs, and other questions like that. Michaela sat on a chair at the table because she didn't like to leave the adults, and listened to the sound of knocking that kept running through the house at odd intervals. Despite Mr Wheeler's assurances that Jack wasn't a frightening ghost, she wasn't sure any more that she wanted to come and live here. She thought of the bedrooms. The way the house was built made it impossible to get from one bedroom to the other by a landing. You would have to come down one dark stairway and through the parlour, the big hall, the dark passage and the kitchen, and then you would have to climb another dark stairway. She thought of making that journey in the middle of the night – through a haunted house – before she could reach her mother, and she felt like crying. But she didn't like to say anything because it would make her seem so cowardly. And her mother would say she was being silly.

'Can I give you a lift to your daughter's, Mr Wheeler?' Mrs Lloyd asked. 'I shall have to go soon, to give Michaela her dinner, but we could easily drop you off—'

'Somebody'll be coming for me,' Mr Wheeler said. 'I don't mind waiting here. I love this house. I wouldn't be leaving it if me bones weren't so old.'

Mrs Lloyd told him not to bother to see them out, but he lifted himself awkwardly from his chair to come to the door with them anyway. Just as they stepped out into the yard, Michaela remembered her tuning-pipes. For the second time since arriving at the house she felt in her pockets for them, and found that they were missing. 'My tuning-pipes! I've lost my tuning-pipes!'

'Oh, those tuning-pipes!' Mrs Lloyd said. 'Run in quick and fetch them.

Do you remember where you left them?'

Michaela stood in the doorway, thinking hard about where she'd last seen the pipes, while her mother explained to Mr Wheeler what it was they'd lost.

'I know where they were!' Michaela said. 'They were on the table in the kitchen. I put them down there when we were eating biscuits.'

'I don't remember seeing them there just now,' Mrs Lloyd said. 'Go on in and get them.'

Michaela looked back at the dark passage and heard, from somewhere within the house, a knocking. She hesitated and looked at her mother. 'Oh, come on then!' her mother said, and went into the house with her.

The tuning-pipes weren't on the table. They didn't seem to be anywhere in the kitchen.

'Hmm,' said Mr Wheeler, who had come back inside with them. 'Jack likes things that make a noise.'

Michaela heard him, and stared at him. Her mother was too busy saying to Michaela, 'Come on, think! Where did you put them down? You must have put them down somewhere. Was it upstairs?'

'Things Jack takes,' Mr Wheeler said, 'usually end up in the hall.' And he gestured towards the door with his stick, inviting Michaela to go with him and look.

They went into the hall together, followed by Mrs Lloyd. There, in the middle of the floor, lay the red box. It was open and the pipes were scattered.

'Honestly, Michaela,' Mrs Lloyd said, as Michaela began to gather the pipes up. 'What a silly place to leave them. What if Mr Wheeler had trodden on one, and it had rolled under his feet?'

Michaela wondered if her mother had been listening to anything Mr Wheeler had said. 'I didn't leave them here. I left them on the table in the kitchen.'

''You're always forgetting where you've left things. You're far too careless.'

Michaela's face was red and she felt very angry. It wasn't fair that she should be told off in front of Mr Wheeler when it hadn't been her fault.

'This is a house where you lose things,' Mr Wheeler said.

As they left the house for the second time, Michaela paused in the doorway of the hall. She held up the red box of tuning-pipes and said to the air, 'They're *mine*.' Then she hurried after Mr Wheeler and her mother.

When she was in the car with her mother, driving back to her grandparents' house, she said, 'Are we going to live there?'

'I think we'll move in at the start of the big holidays,' her mother said. 'That's only a couple of weeks to go.'

'I've changed my mind,' Michaela said. 'I don't want to live in a haunted house.'

'Oh, Mikki! We can't change our minds now we've told Mr Wheeler we'll move in. Besides, I've always wanted to live in a really old house. We're going to.'

'But I'm scared.'

'Don't be silly, Mikki.'

'I'm not being silly. You heard it knocking.'

'Old houses make funny noises.'

'But it knocked back when Mr Wheeler knocked – and when I did!'

'Mr Wheeler was pulling our legs.'

Michaela could see that she was going to be made to move into the haunted house. She thought again about how far apart the bedrooms were. 'I'm not sleeping on my own!'

'We'll talk about it.'

'I'm not!'

Michaela opened her box of tuning-pipes, took out the pipe with the deepest, most lugubrious note, and blew it slowly and gently so that it made an awful, deep, dying noise. She enjoyed it so much that she kept it up all the way home.

CHAPTER THREE

It was twenty-five minutes to ten and Michaela was feeling sleepy. She was sharing an armchair with her mother in the parlour, and they were both comfortable and tired. It had been a hard day. They'd moved into the old house, carrying in boxes of books and a couple of small bookcases, piles of bedding and towels, all their clothes and Michaela's toys, besides the groceries. 'There won't be much to do,' Gran Lloyd had said, 'with you renting the place furnished.' The work had seemed never-ending to Michaela.

Her mother thought so too, and

had said thankfully, 'At least we only have to make up one bed.' Gran Lloyd had agreed with Michaela that it was too much to ask her to sleep on her own at the other end of a strange, haunted house. So Michaela had helped make up the double bed in the little bedroom above the kitchen. 'Handier for the bathroom in the middle of the night as well,' Gran Lloyd had said.

Tiglet had been brought along in her cage, crying loudly all the way, and everyone had to be careful all day long not to leave one of the outer doors open, in case Tiglet ran away and was lost. Not that Tiglet showed much inclination to leave the house. She was much too busy running round the hall and exploring all the other rooms. 'I've never seen a cat settle so quickly,' Gran Lloyd said.

Now, as Michaela and her mother sat in their armchair in front of the television, Tiglet was lying on the hearth and she seemed perfectly happy. Happier than Michaela, who was listening to the sound of someone walking to and fro in the bedroom over their heads. After a while, the footsteps would stop, and taps and knockings would run through the house. Michaela didn't like it, but she didn't want to mention it until her mother did.

'Jack's trying to send us to bed,' Mrs Lloyd said. 'Mr Wheeler said he would.'

'So you do believe in him!'

'I'm joking,' Mrs Lloyd said. 'I've heard noises like that in houses that nobody ever thought were haunted.'

'What are we going to leave for Jack's dinner?'

'Ah . . . ' Mrs Lloyd said. 'He likes bread and cheese, doesn't he? Right, I'll leave him some bread and cheese – and if it turns out he doesn't want it, and leaves it, then I can have it for my breakfast in the morning.'

'You're not supposed to eat the food he leaves because there's no goodness in it!'

'Well, perhaps it won't put any
weight on me then,' Mrs Lloyd said.
'I'll leave him lots of cream buns.'

They sat on in the armchair. Mrs

Lloyd drowsily watched the television. Michaela dozed with her head on her mother's shoulder while Jack was quiet, and lifted her head to listen warily to his knocks when they started. Then the lights went out.

Before either of them had time to move or speak, the lights came on again. 'Mum,' Michaela said, in a shaky voice, 'let's go to bed.'

'Pushed around by a ghost,' Mrs Lloyd said. 'But I'm about ready for bed. I'm whacked. Let me get up.'

Michaela got off her lap. 'We've got to leave his dinner out, remember.'

'Yes, yes, yes,' Mrs Lloyd said. 'Do you think he'll stop knocking and switching lights off while we make his sandwiches?'

Jack did. Mrs Lloyd propped open the door of the parlour with a book, so that Tiglet could wander about in the night, and switched off the parlour light. There was quiet, except for the noise of the traffic on the road outside, as they walked through the hall. The big windows there still let in enough light for them to see their way, but they put the light on in the kitchen.

Mrs Lloyd fetched the loaf and the cheese to the table. 'What am I doing?' she asked herself as she made up two rounds of bread, with cheese, into sandwiches. 'You pour him his milk, Mik.'

'Do you think he'd like squash?' Michaela asked.

'I don't know. Give him squash if you like.'

'I like squash better than milk,' Michaela said, and poured Jack a tall glass of squash. Mrs Lloyd turned a dish over the sandwiches, to keep the dust off them, and draped a clean tea-towel over the glass of squash.

'Good night, Jack,' she said.

When they got upstairs, they found the lights already on in the bathroom and bedroom, as if to welcome them. 'Bags I sleep by the wall,' Michaela said, and was pleased when her mother agreed. Her mother evidently hadn't noticed that the place by the wall was furthest from the window and the door of the bedroom, so whichever way burglars or murderers came in, they'd get her mother first. She took her box of tuning-pipes from her pocket before she started to get undressed, and placed them on the bed, where she could keep her eyes on them every minute while she was taking her clothes off. Then she took them into the bathroom with her and, when she finally climbed into her place in the bed against the wall, she still had them in her hand.

Her mother came and switched off the light before getting into bed and immediately going to sleep – or pretending to. Michaela lay awake. The quietness of the house seemed to rise up from the floor below; she could almost feel the darkness. A car passing on the road outside, and some people shouting on their way back from the pub, seemed very distant noises. And Jack was quiet too. There was no more knocking, no more footsteps. He didn't seem to do much when he had the house to himself.

Michaela opened her box of tuning-pipes and chose one by touch in the dark. She put it to her mouth and blew gently. A sharp 'peep' broke the quiet. She chose another, a much lower, mellower note. She was just about to blow a third when her mother said, in a snorty, muffled voice, 'If you blow another of those damned pipes, I'll chuck them out the window.'

So Michaela shut the box and turned on her side to sleep, still holding the box in her hands. She fell asleep like that.

The room was bright and fresh with sunlight when Michaela woke. She was puzzled at first to find herself in a strange room with her mother lying beside her, reading a book. Her night's sleep had wiped out all memory of the day before, and it took her a minute or two to piece together how she came to be there. Her sleep, she realized, had been deep and undisturbed by ghosts.

'Awake?' her mother asked, when she began to rub her eyes. 'I was having a lie-in, but I suppose we'd better get up.'

Michaela took a bath in the ugly bathtub and dried and dressed herself in the bedroom while her mother washed. From outside came the growling noise of buses and lorries climbing the steep hill, and life seemed so ordinary, and yet the room about her was so strange and new that it was difficult to know how to feel.

She waited for her mother before she went downstairs. She went first, her feet clunking on the wooden steps and between the wooden walls. It was like climbing down into a dark well because the door at the foot of the stairs was shut, and once they'd gone around the twist in the stairs there was no light from above. Michaela was glad to push open the door into the kitchen and see the bright sunlight again.

All the way down the stairs she'd been thinking about the sandwiches and squash they'd left for Jack and as soon as she stepped into the kitchen, she made for the table.

The towel that had covered the glass was lying spread on the table, and the glass was upended on top of it. The squash from the glass had soaked into the towel. The dish had been taken from the plate holding the sandwiches, and the sandwiches themselves had been reduced to crumbs and bits – a large heap of them. It was hard to tell if any of the sandwiches were missing – eaten or otherwise removed.

'Mum! Jack's been! He's had his sandwiches!'

Michaela stared at the plate and the upended glass. She wasn't scared:

somehow a ghost that ate sandwiches seemed much less frightening than the usual ghosts.

'Better than that,' said her mother, in a rather shaky voice. 'He's done the washing-up!'

On the draining board, leaning against each other, were the plates and dishes they had used the night before, and the saucepans, spoons, knives, forks and jugs. From above them, in the air, came a high, sweet peal: a single musical note. Michaela looked up. Jack had her tuning-pipes again – she suddenly remembered falling asleep with them in her hands the night before. They hadn't been in the bed when she'd woken.

Her mother was pulling open the cutlery drawer, with a crash of metal shaken against metal. 'Somebody's got in!' she said.

'No! It's Jack!'

Her mother didn't listen. She took the carving knife from the drawer

and started for the passage. 'Michaela,
stay close by me,' she said.

In the passage they went to the
front and back doors, and Mrs Lloyd

checked both. They were still locked. Almost at a run, Mrs Lloyd went into the hall. Tiglet was lying on the sofa. She looked over her shoulder at them in her best glamour-puss pose, and began to purr. Michaela went to stroke her while her mother examined the windows, and she stayed there while Mrs Lloyd went into the parlour and ran upstairs to the big bedroom. It was while Michaela was sitting on the floor beside the sofa, stroking her cat, that she saw the little red box. It was on the sofa too, close beside Tiglet and almost slipping down the back of the cushions. She grabbed it quickly, looking about her as she did so, almost as if she was snatching it back from a friend who'd sneaked it away. She opened it, and found that a couple of the pipes were missing. Just as she discovered it, another long note was blown in the air, as if Jack was taunting her.

Mrs Lloyd came in from the parlour. 'I can't find any sign of anyone having got in,' she said, still sounding nervous.

'I told you: it's Jack. Mr Wheeler told you he does the washing-up.'

Mrs Lloyd was looking round. 'This place has been tidied too.'

'I thought you said you were glad to have a ghost that'd do the washing-up.'

'When I said that, I didn't really believe it. It's a bit unnerving.'

'Look at Tiglet,' Michaela said. 'She doesn't care about Jack.' Tiglet was licking her fur and purring when she thought about it. Michaela felt comfortable in the house suddenly. Animals were supposed to know when there were ghosts about and be frightened by them, yet Tiglet was happy here. Perhaps she'd feel differently when it was dark again. She'd have to wait and see.

Mrs Lloyd stopped in the middle of the hall, hugging herself. 'I suppose,' she said, 'I'll just have to believe in Jack from now on. How can I not believe in him? That washing-up didn't do itself.'

Then they both raised their heads, startled, as a shower of knocking noises ran round the high walls of the hall, so fast and light that it sounded almost like rain falling. Michaela, crouched by the sofa, and Mrs Lloyd, standing, went on listening long after the knocking stopped.

Then Mrs Lloyd gave a small smile and said, 'Shall we have breakfast?'

They went into the kitchen and Michaela climbed on to a chair at the table while her mother went to the cupboards to fetch the cereal – giving a wary glance at the washing-up on the draining board as she did so.

Michaela saw, on the table in front of her, the two missing tuning-pipes. She opened the little red box and put the pipes back into their places, before putting the box away in her pocket. 'Thank you,' she said aloud.

'What?' her mother asked.

'Nothing,' said Michaela.

CHAPTER FOUR

It was surprising how quickly you could get used to living with a ghost. Mrs Lloyd and Michaela hadn't been in the house a fortnight and already they took Jack for granted, as something that you just had to put up with if you lived there, like the steep stairs and the uneven floors. Mrs Lloyd had even stopped complaining about the expense of leaving something out for Jack every night. After all, she never had to do the washing-up, or pick up all Michaela's toys, books and comics. Even when Michaela had a bath and left the bathroom full of soggy towels, plastic boats and spilt talcum powder, everything was neat the next morning: the towels neatly hung on the rail, the talc somehow swept up, the toy boats gathered tidily into the soap-dish.

It was uncanny; eerie – and yet completely ordinary and normal.

Michaela wasn't afraid to go to bed alone any more, though her mother said she would still sleep in the same room with her for a while. But Michaela felt safe and happy in the house, just as Tiglet did. When she'd been scared of the dark in her gran and grandad's house, and they'd told her that there was no need to worry because they were just downstairs, or in the next room, she'd never felt happy. She'd always thought, what was the use of them being downstairs or in the next room, when the monster might come into *her* room? But Jack was everywhere at once: he filled the house. She was just as much under his protection in the bedroom as her mother was in the parlour.

And usually, before she fell asleep, she heard notes blown in the air on her tuning-pipes. No matter where she put them for safety at night, they were always gone in the morning. She'd find the box, and most of the pipes, in the hall; but Jack usually kept a few of them, sometimes for two or three days before leaving them on the kitchen table, or on one of the windowseats. That was one quarrel Michaela had with Jack: she wished he would leave her tuning-pipes alone and stop stealing them.

Mrs Lloyd didn't get on quite so well with Jack. Even though it was the summer holiday, she still had a lot of work to do, marking books and working out lesson-plans for the next school year. She was used to doing the work in the evenings after Michaela had gone to bed. But Jack liked the house to himself after ten at night. Mrs Lloyd would be sitting at the table in the parlour with her reading lamp angled just as she liked it, happily working away, and she would forget the time. It was easy to ignore Jack's knockings and the occasional musical note, because those noises went on all day. At a few minutes to ten, though, she would hear footsteps walk across the floor of the big bedroom above her head. Backwards and forwards these footsteps would go and, when she ignored them, they would come down the stairs leading into the parlour, and the stair door would open.

'I've got work to do, Jack,' Mrs Lloyd tried saying at first, and she would carry on. Then her reading lamp would switch off, and the work she was trying to concentrate on would vanish into darkness. While she was still trying to defy Jack, she would feel for the lamp in the dark and switch it back on. A minute later, off it would go again.

Once she got up and felt her way across the room to switch the main light on. When she got back to the table, her pen had disappeared. So she took another from her bag. (The one that disappeared was found in the cutlery drawer in the kitchen the next day.)

As quarter past ten approached, Jack became more persistent and bothersome. Mrs Lloyd would begin to feel little sharp tugs at her hair and taps on her shoulder. Papers would slither to the edge of the table and fall off. When she went to pick them up, they would lift, as if on

a breeze, and gust away across the floor. The door from the parlour into the hall would open, as if inviting her to go through it. Mrs Lloyd always found herself on her way to bed before half past ten. It was something else you had to put up with to live in that house. Mr Wheeler, when he came to visit, said that Jack had given him many a thump on the back when he'd come in late from the pub. 'But he's never hurt a soul, Mrs Lloyd, so don't you worry.'

They'd told Gran and Grandad Lloyd a little about Jack. When her grandparents had come visiting, they'd explained the knockings by saying that it was the ghost, and Michaela had tried to tell them about how Jack put all her toys away and washed up at night. But although her gran and grandad pretended to believe, they laughed a lot and didn't really believe. Michaela could tell by the joky way they spoke that they were only playing along with her. So she gave up trying to tell them anything about Jack.

Gran and Grandad Lloyd would always stay with them all day when they came, and while they were sitting round the table for dinner one day, Michaela saw the salt and pepper pots moving. The two little pots circled round each other as if they were dancing – but only while Gran and Grandad Lloyd weren't looking. As soon as they turned to the table, or lifted their heads, the pots stopped. Michaela looked at her mother and saw that Mrs Lloyd had seen the pots moving too. Michaela grinned. It was as if Jack was sharing a joke with them. We know I'm here, he was saying, but *they* don't.

And while they were all sitting in the parlour later, the door to the stairs kept swinging open. Grandad Lloyd got up and went to examine it eventually. 'I could fix this for you,' he said. 'You want it to close properly.'

'No, Dad, leave it,' Mrs Lloyd said. 'I've got to consult Mr Wheeler about all repairs and alterations.'

'But just fixing the door—' Grandad said.

'No, leave it, Dad.'

'Oh, suit yourself,' Grandad Lloyd said. From the air came a deep and rather rude-sounding note – the deepest and least musical of Michaela's tuning-pipes. Michaela and her mother heard it: Gran and Grandad Lloyd seemed not to – but they were both a little deaf.

Tiglet liked Jack. Often she would begin purring when neither Michaela nor Mrs Lloyd were near her. One evening, when she was lying on the hearth, she even rolled on her back and purringly showed her white, furry belly to the empty air. She'd hardly ever roll on her back even for Michaela. Perhaps she liked Jack because he was always about to play with her at the exact moment when she wanted to play. Michaela could rarely manage that, since Tiglet didn't condescend to play very often and, when she did, it was as likely to be in the middle of the night, or for two minutes while Michaela was at the other end of the house, as at any time when Michaela was nearby.

Once, as Michaela walked through the hall, she saw Tiglet crouching and peering at something, and then jumping at it. Michaela walked over and found that the cat was chasing one of her tuning-pipes. The little silver pipe rolled across the wooden floor with a drumming sound and changed direction just as the cat jumped, in a way that a tuning-pipe couldn't possibly do by itself, even on such an uneven floor. Michaela made a grab for the pipe herself and it even evaded her. But she caught it the second time. It felt warm in her hand, as if it had been lying by a window, in sunlight. She took the box of pipes from her pocket and put this lost one back in its place. She counted them and found that there were still three missing. The deepest pipe, with its rude, tuba-like sound had been missing almost since they'd moved into the house.

'They *are* mine,' she said to the wide space of the hall.

Tiglet suddenly ran past her with tail erect and legs scuttling in a blur, and jumped up on one of the window-seats, where she began to purr. Michaela stared at her, annoyed and a little jealous.

Tiglet could see Jack, Michaela was sure. Many times she had seen Tiglet suddenly stiffen and fix wide, staring eyes on some spot where there was nothing to see. And then Tiglet would narrow or blink her eyes, as cats do to their friends, and begin to purr. It was annoying to think that Tiglet knew something she didn't.

So when Mr Wheeler came to see them — as he did, quite often — she asked him, 'What does Jack look like?'

'I wouldn't like to say.'

Michaela was kneeling on a chair by the kitchen table, watching Mr Wheeler hard as he drank his tea. 'Why not?' she asked. 'Is he horrible?'

'No ... I've just never seen him properly. Never heard tell of anybody else who did either.'

'You *have* seen him then?' Michaela said.

'I didn't see him clearly. It was more like a glimpse. I was nailing a carpet down in the big bedroom – I was kneeling in the doorway at the top of the stairs. Well, Jack had been knocking all morning, as usual, but I happened to look down the stairs – and I saw somebody just going around the corner of the stairs, just caught sight of 'em before they disappeared. Well, there wasn't anybody in that part of the house except me, so I figured it must have been Jack I saw. But I only caught a glimpse of his back as he went round the corner. I couldn't say what he looked like from that.'

Michaela thought this over and decided it wasn't good enough. 'What did his back look like?'

'Just – like a back, that's all.'

'How tall was he?' Michaela asked.

'Oh,' Mr Wheeler said, as if surprised that he knew. 'Well, it was a long time ago, but . . . Not very tall, I'd say.'

'Is Jack a little boy then?' Michaela asked eagerly.

'No . . . I wouldn't say he was that small, not from what I saw – though they do say that Jack was a boy who was killed here.'

Michaela's eyes opened wide, and her mouth went round. '*Killed* here?'

'They say he was a boy who used to work for the family that lived here—'

'Your family?' Michaela asked.

'I don't know if it'd be my family. This was a long, long time ago. He worked for the family, and they didn't treat him right. They gave him too much work, and not enough food, and not enough blankets to keep him warm at night, and the end of it all was, he died; and he's haunted the place ever since. That's what they say.'

'Poor Jack!' Michaela said. 'That wasn't fair, to treat him like that!'

'I don't believe it meself,' Mr Wheeler said. 'Look at it this way: if somebody had let you starve and freeze to death, would you come back and do their housework for 'em? *I* wouldn't. I might come back and clank some chains and moan around their beds, but I wouldn't work for 'em like Jack does.'

'What *is* Jack then?'

'I don't know,' Mr Wheeler said. 'I've no idea. He was just built into the house, I think, like the chimneys.'

Michaela frowned. 'I don't know what you mean.'

Mr Wheeler laughed. 'Neither do I, love, neither do I. I'll tell you something, though, something I remember – that time I saw him on the stairs, he had a green hat on ... Or was it red?'

Michaela decided that Mr Wheeler couldn't tell her anything certain about Jack, and that she would just have to find out for herself.

She wanted to know what Jack looked like. She wanted to be the person who saw him plainly, and could tell people what a ghost looked like. Just think, she'd be the only person who'd ever seen a ghost for certain. People would want to interview her; she'd be in the newspapers. She could write a book about it.

She thought of stretching cotton threads across the big bedroom where Jack walked, and across the stairway leading down from it. Even if Jack broke the threads, she still wouldn't know what he looked like, of course, but she had read of ghost-hunters doing things like that.

'No,' her mother said, when asked if she would help. 'How are you going to stick the threads to the walls? Whatever you use, you might damage the wallpaper, and Mr Wheeler wouldn't like that, would he? Tell you what,' she added, when it seemed that Michaela might sulk, 'you can spread some flour on the floor, provided you get it up. Then you'll be able to see his footsteps, won't you?'

So Michaela spent some of her

money on a small bag of plain flour, and enjoyed spreading it on the floor of the big bedroom. She started near the window and walked backwards towards the door and the stairs, tossing the flour over the floor in handfuls. It landed with soft puffs, and drifted in white clouds, until she was all white herself. It was wonderful to have permission to do it, but she had to wash and change afterwards.

Much later, that night, as she sat in the parlour with her mother, she heard Jack's footsteps crossing and recrossing the floor. She didn't like to go up there at night, but she could imagine herself going into the room the first thing the next morning. And there would be the footprints in the flour. Huge, flat-footed footprints, perhaps – or maybe little, goaty-hoofed ones?

But the next morning, when she ran up the stairs and pushed open the door at the top, she saw a polished wooden floor in the sun. It was swept bare of any trace of flour. She walked over it, and she couldn't see even a speck of flour caught between the planks. The flour, and any footprints it had held, had all been swept up.

'Well, that's Jack for you,' Mrs Lloyd said, when Michaela told her. 'You make a mess, he tidies it up – bless him!'

Tiglet sometimes had mad moments, when she would rush

about, leaping on the furniture and chasing her own tail or scraps of paper. Jack sometimes had similar fits, when he would knock on walls, open and shut doors, switch lights on and off, throw cushions about, and keep it up for a whole morning or evening. Michaela wondered whether, if she could keep up with him at these times, she might catch a glimpse of him. Surely, she thought, he wasn't invisible all the time? When he was knocking in the hall or passage, and they were in the kitchen, surely he wasn't invisible then? Why should he bother, when they couldn't see him anyway? After all, if Mr Wheeler had looked up from his hammering a moment earlier, he'd have seen Jack clearly instead of just catching sight of him going round the corner. She had to try to be in the right place at the right time.

So she began trying to catch Jack. If he started to knock in the evenings, when she was home, she would

take off her shoes so as not to make
any noise, and run after the knockings. She'd dash up the stairs to the
big bedroom, where she often found
the spy-hole open — and then the
knocking would be from downstairs.
Down she'd run — and the knocking
would be upstairs again. Sometimes
he would lead her from the parlour to
the other end of the house, to the
kitchen — and then he would be
knocking upstairs in her bedroom, or
in the hall. However quietly she ran,
or however quickly, she never, never
caught him. Once the door of the hall
slammed shut in her face as she was
running to the kitchen, where the
knocking was going on, and when
she tried to open it, she couldn't. The
knob wouldn't turn. It was as if someone was holding it from the other
side. She struggled with it until she
was hot, and then the handle was
suddenly released, the door flew
open, and she went staggering back.
Immediately the knocking began

behind her, in the parlour. When she picked herself up and ran there breathlessly, the knocking switched to the hall.

'Why don't you give up?' her mother asked her. 'How do you expect to catch whatever-it-is?'

'I want to know what he looks like!'

'I know everything about him I want to know,' Mrs Lloyd said. 'I've got to admit he exists; and if I follow the rules, I get my washing-up done for me. I'm happy to leave it at that.'

Michaela thought this very cowardly of her mother. Fancy not wanting to find out everything you could about something as mysterious and fascinating as Jack! But it became clear that while she never knew where Jack would knock next, he knew perfectly well where she was, and could make her chase him all round the house, or run up and down the stairs seven times. It was fun at first, like playing with Tiglet. It was fun to play with a creature so different to yourself. It was as close as you could get to talking with an animal – or a ghost. But she quickly tired of the game because she hadn't any chance at all of winning. It didn't matter how cleverly or cunningly she played, it seemed she was never, even by accident, going to get a look at Jack. A change of plan was called for.

It was the day after she'd decided this that, while eating breakfast, she discovered that one of her back teeth was loose. She stopped eating because she hated the way the tooth wobbled when she chewed: it made her feel slightly sick. Losing a tooth always made her glum because she dreaded that it was going to hurt when it came out.

'Never mind, you'll get something from the tooth fairy,' her mother said when she told her.

That didn't make Michaela feel much better. Nothing would until the tooth was out.

'Tell you what,' her mother said.

'Why don't I drive you over to your gran's, and you can stay there while I do the shopping? You could go and see your friends.'

'No,' Michaela said. Her mother would tell her gran about the loose tooth, and her gran would make a big fuss and would keep offering to pull it out.

'Well, come on then. You'll have to come shopping with me.'

'Don't want to. I want to stay here.'

'I can't leave you on your own.'

'Why not?' Michaela asked. 'I know everything I've not got to do. I won't play with matches or open the door to anyone. Anyway, Jack would stop anything happening.'

'Jack!' her mother said. They had a long argument, but Michaela eventually won it because Mrs Lloyd didn't want to drag her round the shops if she was moaning about having to come along all the time. Mrs Lloyd went off to the shops after giving her a long list of things that

Michaela wasn't to do. 'And if you think of something to do and you're in any doubt about whether or not you should do it – don't!' was the last thing she said before going out of the door.

Michaela knew what she was going to do. She went through the hall and parlour and climbed halfway up the stairs to the big bedroom, to the place just above where they turned the corner; and she sat down. There she was going to sit, all day long, until she saw Jack. She could see light from the open door at the bottom shining on the wall at the corner. If she looked up, she could see light shining through the open door at the top. In the middle, where she was, the light was dim, and the place smelt of wood and dust.

The stairs themselves were worn. Hard ridges stood up from the wood, and the steps sloped to one side, or bowed in the middle. They were very hard to sit on, and her flesh, pinched between her bones and the wood,

began to feel bruised. Every now and again, she'd poke her loose tooth with her tongue, feel queasy when she felt it move in the gum, and wish she hadn't done it. The house around her was silent. There were no sounds made by her mother and, unusually, no knocking or footsteps. It was more uncomfortable on the stairs than she'd realized it would be. Perhaps sitting there for the whole day was a bit much. Perhaps she'd just sit there until her mother came back.

Then, from the parlour at the foot of the stairs, came a long, sweet note – her favourite of all the notes her tuning-pipes played. She was annoyed immediately. Again! Jack wouldn't leave her pipes alone! And her favourite one. The note was repeated, and she knew it was meant to taunt her.

She slipped down the stairs on her bottom, as quietly as she could. She wanted to get, very quietly, to where she could see into the parlour. Her mind was showing her pictures of what she might see. Jack, sitting in one of the parlour armchairs, his green, or possibly red, hood on his head, the pipe in his mouth. But she couldn't make up her mind what Jack himself should look like. In the few moments it took her to slip down the stairs she imagined him as looking like Mr Wheeler; as looking like herself; as looking – for some reason – like a fat, bald man. And like a goblin she'd once seen drawn in a book. None of these seemed right. And when she was able to see a section of the parlour through the stair door, there was no-one there. She went right to the bottom of the stairs and looked round the whole parlour. No-one. She was rather glad that the goblin she'd imagined wasn't there, but she was disappointed too.

From behind her, from about half-way up the stairs, where she'd been sitting, came the long, sweet note again. Suddenly mad, Michaela ran back up the stairs as if she was running to hit someone who had been teasing her. There was no-one on the stairs, but something fell, struck the steps and went falling down them with a sound that was at once a clank and a chime. She turned and chased it, and picked up the thing as it reached the bottom of the stairs. It was one of her tuning-pipes: the one that played the note she had heard. As always when Jack had been playing with a pipe, it was warm to the touch.

She held the little pipe firmly in her hand and took the box holding the others from her pocket. She counted the pipes in the box and found, with surprise, that they were all there except one – the one she now had in her hand. As she sat on the bottom step, with the box of pipes in one hand and the single pipe in the other, she heard her mother open the front door and call. An idea came to her. She got up and ran outside. Her mother was unloading groceries from the boot of the car and hadn't locked the doors yet. Michaela climbed into the front seat and opened the glove compartment. She put the tuning-pipes inside and shut the compartment again. Then she got out of the car and helped her mother with the groceries.

'They're my pipes!' she shouted as she went into the house. Jack had never been known to work any of his tricks outside the house, so the pipes should be safe from him in the car. It would mean that she couldn't play with them either, except when she was outside, but she felt in a spiteful mood. She felt it was worth having to give up the pipes for most of the time, if Jack couldn't have them either when he was so fond of them. If he won't let me see what he looks like, she thought, why should I do him any favours?

She half expected to hear hammering, or a door slamming, as a reply, but there was no sound. Indeed, for the rest of the day, there was little sign of Jack being about. No footsteps, no knockings, no doors opening or shutting. With no sounds to guide her, Michaela felt she had less chance than ever of seeing Jack. It wasn't fair, she thought. He'd let Mr Wheeler see him – well, nearly. Why wouldn't he let her get a look at him?

That evening, Mrs Lloyd made them beans on toast for tea. She made Jack's porridge at the same time and set it on the draining board. Jack didn't seem to mind his porridge being cold.

Mrs Lloyd quickly finished her meal, but Michaela had hardly started hers. 'What's the matter with it?' her mother asked.

'I don't like chewing. My tooth keeps moving.'

'Oh, the fuss you make about a loose tooth. Give a good bite and it'll come out, and all be over.'

'No,' Michaela said.

'You'll still have it a fortnight from now, the way you nurse it.'

'I don't care.'

'Your tea will be cold before you've finished.'

'It is cold,' Michaela said.

'Well, I've got work to do; I'm going to leave you to get on with it.' And Mrs Lloyd went through into the parlour.

Michaela went on slowly with her meal, taking tiny bites and chewing them at the opposite side of her mouth to the loose tooth. Then she left it, because the beans had gone cold and the toast soggy. She still felt hungry, but she didn't want to eat because of the loose tooth; and she felt miserable too. It was then that she noticed Jack's bowl of porridge on the draining board.

She left her seat, took the salt and pepper pots from the table and salted the porridge until it was white, and peppered it until it was brown, and then she mixed it all in until it

looked almost like ordinary porridge. She kept looking round as she did it, as if she might see Jack watching her. She couldn't be sure that he wasn't watching her. But there was no sound, and nothing moved.

She ran through into the parlour then, singing, to show her mother that she was thinking of nothing at all except the song she was singing and hadn't done anything that she shouldn't have done. Her mother took no notice.

It served Jack right, Michaela thought. Two could play at being spiteful.

CHAPTER FIVE

Michaela woke in the night, with the kind of jump that wakes you from a nightmare. It was a warm night and, between her mother and the wall, she was too hot. She lay in the hot dark, her hair sticking to her brow, her heart beating too fast and a fluttering in her ears, and she listened.

A moment later there came a sound, and she jumped so violently at the shock of it that she lifted herself from the pillow. The sound seemed to come from the end of the bed, and it was as if a tall, thick-sided, heavy wardrobe had abruptly tipped over and smacked its full weight on the wooden floor with the flat of its doors: a gigantic crash that echoed through the room and shook the walls and floor. Her heart felt as if it had hit the ceiling and then crashed back into her body, where it continued to bang between her ribs.

The beating of her heart was taking up so much room in her chest that she hardly had any space left to take a breath. She lay down in the shelter of her mother's back and made herself small and quiet. Beside her, Mrs Lloyd moved, sighed, and woke. Still lying stiff and quiet, holding her breath, Michaela could feel and hear her mother turning and twisting in the bed, and pushing herself up on one elbow.

Then the crash came again, just as loud, just as impossible. Another wardrobe had fallen exactly where the first one had – where no wardrobe stood in any case. Michaela heard her mother yell, and then was closing her eyes against bright light.

Squinting and daring to peer out from the sheet, she saw that her mother had jumped out of bed and switched on the light. Mrs Lloyd was staring at the spot where the crash had come from.

Her mother being awake gave Michaela the courage to sit up in bed and look too. There was no wardrobe at the end of the bed, either standing or fallen. It was a small room, and there wasn't room for a wardrobe to fall. There was hardly room for one to stand. Looking round the room Michaela saw that nothing at all had fallen. The room was just the same as it had always been.

Mrs Lloyd was standing by the light switch, her hand over her heart. Breathlessly, she said, 'What the hell was that?' Seeing her mother look so shocked, and hearing her sound so frightened, was scary for Michaela. She jumped out of bed too, and ran to hold on to her mother. She even whimpered a little bit.

'Now it's nothing to be scared of,'
Mrs Lloyd was saying, when they
heard someone running up the stairs
to their room, someone running

lightly as if in soft shoes. Michaela felt her mother go rigid. Then, on the closed door of their room came one blow, as if struck by a fist.

Michaela heard her mother swallow and realized that her mother was very scared indeed, more scared than Michaela had ever known her be. Michaela was scared too, but with a difference. Michaela knew exactly what was going on, and why that blow had been struck on the door. It was because she had done that sneaky and spiteful thing and spoilt Jack's dinner.

Mrs Lloyd spoke quietly. 'Michaela,' she said. 'Go into the bathroom and lock yourself in.'

'Why?' Michaela said.

'Do as you're told. Lock yourself in.'

'It's not a murderer,' Michaela said. 'It's Jack. He's angry.'

Her mother pushed her towards the bathroom. 'Do as you're told!'

Michaela went over to the bathroom, she even opened the door, but she didn't go in. She looked back and saw her mother yank open the door to the stairs. Even though they had heard the footsteps come up the stairs and stop outside the door, there was no-one there. Michaela had known there wouldn't be. The noises were all made by Jack.

Mrs Lloyd leaned out and looked down the stairs. She looked back at Michaela with a frightened face and said, 'I told you to go into the bathroom.' Then she looked down the stairs again. After a moment of hesitation, she started down them. Her white nightgown glimmered palely on the darkness of the stairs.

Michaela darted across the room after her, waited at the top of the stairs until her mother had gone into the kitchen, and then went down after her.

Mrs Lloyd had switched the light on in the kitchen and, under the flat, yellow light, she was standing by the table. She jumped and turned as

Michaela came in, and spoke her daughter's name angrily. Michaela ran over to her anyway. Her mother was standing by a mess on the floor: pieces of broken dish, and something that had been in it. Michaela realized that it was Jack's porridge: the porridge she had spoilt with salt and pepper. It had been thrown on the floor and smashed.

The invisible wardrobe fell again, and both mother and daughter leapt off the floor in fright and held tight to each other. This time it sounded as if the wardrobe had crashed down in the corner of the kitchen, on to the hard stone tiles – but there was nothing, nothing at all to cause such a sound.

'I'm sorry!' Michaela shouted, her voice rising sharp and high, and wavering.

The kitchen door opened violently and dashed against the wall. Mrs Lloyd, still holding Michaela, staggered and cried out. In stumbling, they fell against the kitchen table and bruised themselves. 'Pushed!' Mrs Lloyd said. 'I was pushed.'

They were pushed again as soon as they moved away from the table, pushed towards the open door and the dark passage beyond. There was another crashing noise – the wooden drawer had been pulled from the table and had fallen with a thump on the tiles, followed by many, many crashes and clashes of knives, forks and spoons. The noise seemed to echo in their heads for minutes – and before they were clear of it, things were flying through the air towards them. Things that, when they hit them, hurt. Knives, forks and spoons.

Michaela's arm was hurt by her mother's grip on it. Her mother dragged her out of the kitchen and into the passage. Knives, forks, spoons, shot through the kitchen door and thumped against the wall of the passage, the thumps echoing down its length.

'Oh, my God,' Mrs Lloyd said, ducking and holding Michaela tightly to her. She kept saying it, over and over, as if saying it was going to be some help.

The light in the hall switched on, and they saw that the door in to the hall was standing open. Then a dark shape blocked out the light in the doorway. Someone was coming out of the hall. Michaela felt a great block of fear rise sharply into her throat, sealing off her breath. With a flap, like a bat, the someone came rattling through the doorway at them, touched them, making them both cry out – and then fell at their feet. It was Mrs Lloyd's raincoat.

Mrs Lloyd took Michaela by the hand and made for the front door. She put Michaela between the door and herself, and stared back down the passage in terror as she felt in the pocket of her hung-up jacket for her keys. At the other end of the passage, by the back door, the invisible ward-

robe fell again, but though Mrs Lloyd jumped and shivered, she kept hold of the keys. She even turned her back on the passage while she unlocked the front door. 'Run to the car,' she said to Michaela.

'Tiglet!' Michaela said.

'O-oh!' Mrs Lloyd made to go forward to the car, half turned back, turned for the car again, then stopped. 'Go to the car,' she said. 'I'll find Tiglet.'

She pushed Michaela out of the front door and ran down the passage calling, 'Puss, puss! Tiggie!'

Michaela stood outside the front door in the dark, looking into the yellowness of the lit passage. Even though it was summer, it was cold out there in her pyjamas. She saw her mother come hurrying out of the kitchen like a ghost in her nightgown, and vanish into the hall. She ran back into the house herself, following her mother.

It felt unsafe in the hall. The room was so big; it held so much space, and made the light from the two little electric bulbs dangling from the beams seem so weak. Mrs Lloyd was standing in the middle of the floor, quite still, as if she'd just heard something. Michaela ran across the floor to her and caught hold of her hand. Mrs Lloyd gripped it tightly. Together they crept across the floor towards the sofa and armchairs, as if they were trying not to disturb someone. The house was silent, as silent as a house should be in the middle of the night, though all the lights were on.

Tiglet was curled up on the end of the sofa, her white paws over her eyes, as if to keep out the light. She was fast asleep. They had time to see so much before the parlour door at the other end of the hall opened and then slammed shut so hard that they felt the boards beneath their feet tremble. Tiglet didn't so much as twitch an ear. It was as if – with her keen, cat hearing – she had heard none of the noise.

One of Mrs Lloyd's little bookcases stood near the parlour door. As they were looking towards the door, they saw the bookcase topple and fall as if it had been thrown over. The books fell out on to the floor, and the bookcase landed on top of them. And then a book came flying at them, pages flapping and showering from it – a whole flock of books. Mrs Lloyd, still gripping Michaela's hand tightly, ran from the hall. Michaela didn't need to be dragged – she was running just as fast.

The front door at the end of the passage was still standing open, and they ran through it into the chill darkness. Behind them, the door slammed.

They ran into the cold metal sides of the car and leaned against it. 'You've got the keys?' Mrs Lloyd asked.

Michaela gave them to her and went round to the passenger door. A moment later, they were both inside the car with the doors locked. They sat there, waiting for their hearts to slow down. Light from the kitchen window fell over the bonnet of the car, and light from the hall windows fell over the drive behind the car. The curtains had been opened.

Mrs Lloyd reached into the back of the car and pulled an old knitted blanket over to the front seats. She wrapped them both in it. Neither of them spoke, though Michaela opened the glove compartment and took out the little red box of tuning-pipes. She selected the pipe with the sweetest, prettiest note and sat blowing it softly. Then she took out a pipe with a similar sweet sound and blew them alternately and together. The sounds were soothing. Even Mrs Lloyd must have thought so, because she didn't tell her to be quiet. From the house, as far as they could tell, came no sound at all.

After what seemed to Michaela a very long time, Mrs Lloyd said, in an almost normal voice, 'I've gone right off ghost stories.'

'What are we going to do?' Michaela asked then.

'Tonight? Stay here, I suppose, until it's light.'

'And then what?' Michaela asked.

'I think – tell Mr Wheeler that we don't want to rent his house any more.'

'Oh, no Mum! I like living here.'

'Well, so do I, but – but this is

ridiculous! I mean, it can't be happening – it shouldn't be happening! I can put up with a lot – I can put up with feeling like a fool because I'm making porridge for a ghost. I can put up with having to go to bed at ten because something I don't really believe in won't let me stay up any longer. Even Cinderella had until midnight! But I won't put up with being chased out of my own house in the middle of the night – and having knives thrown at me—' Mrs Lloyd stopped and gripped the steering-wheel tightly. 'I could get very silly about this.'

'It's only this once,' Michaela said.

'How do we know? The thing might make a habit of it.'

'It won't happen again,' Michaela said.

'It won't! We're moving out.'

Michaela was quiet after that, sitting with her feet dangling above the floor of the car. She wondered what would happen if they did move out. What if Mr Wheeler couldn't find anyone else to live in the house? There would be no-one to feed Jack. And Jack would have no-one to tease or work for. She leaned her head against her mother's shoulder so that she could look out through the windows of the car and see the lit windows of the house. Jack did have a bad temper, she thought. She could understand him being angry at what she'd done, but he'd gone a bit far.

She fell asleep, and when she woke, she felt strange. She was unusually cold and stiff, and wasn't sure where she was. The light was grey and pearly, washing the colour out of everything.

'That's the last of the sunrise,' her mother said, pointing to some pink and yellow streaks in the sky.

'I'm cold,' Michaela said. Her mother turned the engine on, and the heater. Michaela leaned on her mother, waiting to feel warm and gradually becoming aware of other feelings. 'I'm hungry.'

'All the food's in the house.'

'We could go to Gran's.'

'In our nightclothes?' Mrs Lloyd asked. 'And what would we say? "The ghost's thrown us out."?' After another few minutes, Mrs Lloyd turned off the engine and said, 'We're going back inside. I'm not going to be sitting out here when the milkman comes.'

Mrs Lloyd got out of the car and marched over to the door of the house in her bare feet. Michaela slid over into the driving seat, and from there on to the drive, following not quite so bravely. It was very cold in the early morning, though. If they could go into the house long enough to get dressed, and get something to eat and drink, she'd feel a lot happier.

Mrs Lloyd had her keys and opened the door. She peered into the passage cautiously. No sound came from the house, and nothing came flying at her. She slipped inside, reaching behind to draw Michaela after her.

Together they crept down the passage towards the kitchen. Under her breath, Michaela was saying, 'I'm sorry, Jack, I'm sorry, I'm sorry . . . '

They reached the kitchen without having heard any wardrobe crashes, or doors slamming, or having anything thrown at them. The light was still on, but the cutlery had all been gathered up and the drawer that held it was back in place. Only the smashed bowl and spoiled porridge still lay on the floor.

Mrs Lloyd opened the stair door and peered up the stairs. She couldn't decide whether to send Michaela up first, or lead the way herself. There wasn't room for them to go side by side. In the end, she sent Michaela up first, but walked close behind her, holding on to her.

They were allowed to reach their bedroom without anything happening. 'Right,' said Mrs Lloyd. 'We won't wash. Just get some clothes on as quick as you can – put 'em on over your pyjamas.' Mrs Lloyd was herself pulling jeans and jumper on over her nightgown.

Once dressed, after a fashion, they hurried down to the kitchen again. There, Mrs Lloyd began gathering together bread and cheese, as if to take them out to the car, but she suddenly stopped. 'You need something hot,' she said to Michaela, 'so we're staying here.' She spoke the last part loudly, as if she was speaking to Jack. 'Why should we run away?' she said. 'Sit down at the table. I'll make some porridge.'

From the far end of the house came a distant crash, as if the invisible but huge wardrobe had toppled over in the parlour. 'Go on, go on,' Mrs Lloyd said, and pulled out the cutlery drawer with a metallic rattle to get a spoon. 'We're staying.'

They stayed and ate porridge and drank cocoa which Mrs Lloyd made especially for Michaela; but Jack didn't leave them entirely alone.

After they'd finished breakfast, Mrs Lloyd cleaned up the broken bowl and spilled porridge; but as soon as it was cleaned up, another bowl came sailing from the dresser and smashed on the floor. And when Mrs Lloyd had recovered from the shock and collected up the new broken pieces, another bowl was thrown down and smashed.

'Doesn't seem like he wants it cleared up, does it?' Mrs Lloyd asked nervously. 'I suppose I'd better leave that mess, or we won't have a bowl left in the house.'

This wasn't all. The kitchen door opened as often as Mrs Lloyd closed it. Bangs, thumps and crashes came from all parts of the house, sometimes distant and muffled, sometimes startlingly loud. Several times the noise of the traffic on the road outside became unusually noisy and, on going out into the passage to find out why, they would see the front door standing open. Apologizing, it seemed, hadn't done any good. Michaela got a bowl, filled it with cornflakes, added milk, and placed it in the middle of the kitchen table. When her mother asked why, she said, 'It's for Jack.' Her mother sighed, and tutted, but didn't take the bowl away.

'I'll make us a shepherd's pie for lunch,' Mrs Lloyd said, and started to peel potatoes at the sink. Michaela was bored, sitting in the kitchen, but she didn't want to leave her mother alone in the house, or to go by herself to any other part of the house. She asked if she could cut the potatoes in pieces and drop them into the saucepan.

When the potatoes were boiling, Mrs Lloyd decided to make an apple crumble for pudding. Michaela thought that all this cooking was just to give her mother something to do, but she was happy to rub the fat into the flour for the crumble's top, while her mother peeled and sliced apples. So they spent the morning, both feeling like nervous strangers in the house, their voices a little too sharp to each other's ears, trying to pretend that they couldn't hear the noises Jack was making.

They both started when someone knocked on the door of the kitchen, and a voice said, 'Hello.' Michaela dropped the knife she was using to chop carrots to go with the shepherd's pie. But it was only Mr Wheeler.

'Excuse me,' he said, 'but the front door was standing open so I came in.'

'That's your precious Jack,' Mrs Lloyd said, quite angrily, but then added, 'Oh, Mr Wheeler, I apologize, but we've had such a night! Come and sit down, please. Mikki, get Mr Wheeler a cup. Would you like shepherd's pie and apple crumble, Mr Wheeler? We'd be glad of the company of somebody who's used to this house!'

While they finished preparing the vegetables for dinner, Mr Wheeler drank tea, and Mrs Lloyd and Michaela told him of what had happened during the night. Jack, from the moment Mr Wheeler had walked in, limited his activities to the occasional knock.

'I've never known him behave like that before,' Mr Wheeler said. 'Not in all my life. What did you do?'

Michaela looked down at the wooden table top and played with a little curly bit of bright carrot peeling. Mrs Lloyd tipped back her head, laughed, threw wide her arms and said, 'What did we do? I don't believe this. It's happening, but I don't believe it.'

'You did put his food out, didn't you?' Mr Wheeler asked.

'Yes,' Mrs Lloyd said, with exaggerated patience. 'Because I'd promised you, because it was a quaint tradition, because, God help me, my washing-up was done, I put its food out every single night, faithfully, without fail.'

'Then I don't know,' Mr Wheeler said. 'I've never known—' As he was saying this, he looked across the table into Michaela's face. He stopped

speaking and looked thoughtful. Michaela, her guilty conscience smarting, blushed and looked down at the table top again.

'Perhaps it's *us* it doesn't like,' Mrs Lloyd said.

'No, no,' Mr Wheeler said. 'Jack likes you, or you'd never have settled down so quickly. But I remember another story about Jack. A long time ago here, a long, long time ago, they used to make their own cloth, and they used to dye it. You know what they used to use to fix the dye so it wouldn't wash out again?'

He was looking at Michaela, so she said, 'No.' Her blush, which had been fading, grew hotter again. She was sure, from the way he looked at her, that Mr Wheeler guessed something of what she'd done.

'Well, I hope your mother won't mind me telling you this, but it's historical, it's proper historical fact. They used piddle.' Michaela stared and then began to giggle. Her mother frowned at her. 'They used to keep it in buckets until it had gone stale,' Mr Wheeler went on. 'Now the story goes that there used to be a boy who worked here, and because everybody else had so much work to do, he was given the job of making sure that Jack's food was always left for him. But one night he played a trick on Jack. You know what he did?'

Warily, afraid that Mr Wheeler was about to tell tales on her, Michaela shook her head.

'He put the old stale piddle that was meant for the dyeing in Jack's bowl instead of milk. And off he went to bed, laughing, thinking what a good joke it was.'

Michaela pulled a face. *That* was much worse than putting pepper and salt in his porridge, she thought.

'And you know what Jack did to him?' Mr Wheeler asked.

'Made a lot of noise?' Michaela said. 'Woke them all up in the night?'

'No,' Mr Wheeler said. 'In the middle of the night he dragged that boy out of bed, and he thumped him, and pinched him, and pulled out his hair. Chased him all round the house, he did, with the boy screaming blue murder. Black and blue he was by the time Jack'd finished.'

From upstairs came a heavy thump, and Michaela's heart began to beat a little fast again. It seemed Jack hadn't served her and her mother so badly after all, compared to what he *could* have done.

'And that wasn't all,' Mr Wheeler said. 'Because the gaffer of the house, he was so scared that Jack was going to leave and take all the luck with him, that when he found out what the boy had done, he sacked him, kicked him off the farm. And then the gaffer had to make it up to Jack.'

'How did he do that?' Michaela said, trying to sound as if she didn't particularly want to know.

'He made sure that Jack got the best they had for the next month, to make up for the boy's trick. He set it out himself: the best beer, the best bread. Butter, honey, porridge made with milk by the missis herself. And Jack stayed on. But because of what that boy did, Jack might have gone away to another farm and taken all the luck with him.' And Mr Wheeler looked at Michaela hard, as if he was asking: Do you understand?

Michaela thought that she did.

CHAPTER SIX

Michaela wanted to be by herself and think. She left her mother and Mr Wheeler talking in the kitchen and, because she didn't want to be on her own in any other part of the house, she went outside. The car doors were still unlocked, and she climbed into the driving seat where she sat moving the gear-stick and pretending that she was changing gear. When she tired of that, she took her tuning-pipes out of the glove compartment and blew on each one, first at random and then in order, from the deepest to the highest. Her thoughts were of Jack, even though she didn't know what he – or it – was, or what he – or it – looked like, or even if he – or it – looked like anything at all.

The house was a very old one. The hall might even be seven hundred years old, her mother had said once. Michaela tried to imagine seven hundred years passing by. She couldn't, of course. She'd only lived eight, and that seemed a long time. It always seemed an agonizingly long wait from one Christmas to another, and that was only one year. Multiply that long, long wait for Christmas by one hundred, and then multiply that by seven, and you had the time Jack had spent in the house – but Michaela couldn't hold so huge a number in her head. It made her giddy. Perhaps something like an oak tree, something very, very big and strong and slow, could know what seven hundred years was like . . . or something not seen in this world, like Jack.

All that time Jack had guarded the

house, so Mr Wheeler said, and brought it luck. He must have always worked for the people who lived in it, whoever they were. There must have been so many of them in seven hundred years. And all those people must always have kept their side of the bargain, setting out food for him at night. She thought of all those people, lines and lines of them going away from her into the past, their clothes getting stranger and stranger like the drawings in history books. How many of them had there been? Thinking of it made her feel dizzy again, and she had to stop and concentrate on the sounds of the pipes for a while.

Jack had always liked the pipes; and she'd taken them away from him and hidden them in the car, just so that he couldn't have them. And he'd never taken them all away from her, except when she was asleep. At other times he'd only ever taken one or two. She supposed a little food, and a turn with the pipes now and then wasn't much to ask for guarding the house, bringing them luck, and doing most of their housework. She began to feel sad and ashamed about what she'd done.

That trick the boy had played on him must have been a nasty shock. No wonder Jack had been so angry to find his porridge full of salt and pepper. And what if the trick she'd played made Jack go away? Where would he go? There weren't any other old houses nearby. There were only new houses, where the people would be frightened of him.

I was wrong, she suddenly decided. *I shouldn't have done it. And now I've got to say sorry, not just because I hope to stop Jack being angry, but because I really am sorry. I've got to make up for what I did.*

She went back into the house by the back door, and walked the length of the passage to where their coats hung. On the wall above her head there sounded three knocks. In the pocket of her coat she found the little purse where she kept her pocket money. Her mother and Mr Wheeler were still talking in the kitchen as she slipped out of the house again.

She walked away from the house, down the steep hill and past the pub to the row of local shops. She went into the paper shop and stood in front of the sweet counter, deciding how

she should spend her money. She would spend it all, she decided, on sweets.

There were other people coming in, buying papers and magazines, so she had plenty of time to choose. Some cola bottles, she decided, and some of those flying saucers, filled with sherbet. Some bright red cherry kisses, and some sweethearts. Liquorice bootlaces, red and black, and three of those chewy jellies shaped like lizards. The shopkeeper weighed them all out, and she paid. She got two pence change.

On the way home, she did eat a sweetheart and one of the cherry kisses, but that was all. She stopped outside the house and tried the car door. It was still unlocked – she'd have to remind her mother. But it meant she was able to get the tuning-pipes out of the glove compartment.

She went back into the house by the back door and passed by the door to the kitchen, where she could hear her mother and Mr Wheeler still talking. Her mother heard her and called out, 'Michaela! Come and have your dinner now.'

'In a minute!' she shouted back, and went into the hall.

She paused for a moment at the door, searching the big room with her eyes. There was silence, except for the slight thump Tiglet made as she jumped down from a windowseat and came towards her, purring. Slowly, Michaela went into the room and began to cross it towards the parlour. Nothing moved and there was no sound, not even Jack's usual knocking.

Halfway across she began to feel very uneasy. She seemed so far away from the kitchen and company. She stopped and looked all round her. She couldn't see anything, but then she never had seen Jack. One more step, she said to herself.

She took one more step, and then another and another, until she reached the door of the parlour. She went in carefully. The room, as ever, was pleasant and peaceful, and full of sunshine from the big window. But it was quiet. She couldn't hear anything of her mother and Mr Wheeler any more, they were so far away.

Tiptoeing, she crossed the parlour towards the stairs, but hesitated before she opened the stair door. These were the stairs where Mr Wheeler had once caught a glimpse of Jack. What if she opened the door and Jack was behind it, and his face was horrible – a monster's face?

It took a lot of courage to open the door, and it seemed a long time before she could make herself do so. When she did, there was nothing behind the door except the stairs and the dimness. Then she felt that she'd always known it would be like that. But she peered timidly round the corner of the stairs before she went up any further. Her heart seemed to be knocking on her ears, it was pumping her blood so fast.

At the top was another closed door, leading into the big bedroom, and she stopped again. The big bedroom was where Jack was heard walking most often. She always thought that, if he lived anywhere in the house, it was in that room. At last, remembering that her mother was waiting for her and might come looking for her before she'd done what she'd decided she had to do, she pushed the door open hard.

And there was the big bedroom, sunny and polished and almost empty of furniture. It was just as old and strange, and just as ordinary as it always was. She'd known, really, that it would look like that, despite her fears.

Except that the spy-hole was open again. It nearly always was, no matter how often it was closed.

Michaela went over to the room's

fireplace and, kneeling down, placed the white bags of sweets on the hearth. Beside them she placed the little flock-covered red box full of silver tuning-pipes.

Still kneeling there, she said, aloud, 'Jack – these are for you, Jack, to say I'm sorry. It was only pepper and salt I put in your food, but I shouldn't have done it anyway, and I won't ever do anything like it again, I promise. So can we be friends again, please? Or, if you won't be friends with me, be friends with Mum again, because she didn't do anything. She didn't know. You can have the pipes as well, because I know you like them. That's to show I really want to be friends.'

She remained kneeling, trying to think if there was anything else to say. There was no answer of any kind, not even a knock. The sunlight shone on the floorboards and reflected from the dressing-table mirror on to the wall, and if it hadn't been for a shivery feeling over her skin, and a sensation in her back that made her want to twitch her shoulders together, she would have said that the room was empty except for her. But it wasn't empty. It didn't feel empty.

She stood and waited a little longer, looking round the room as if she expected to see some sign that her message had been heard and understood – and then she suddenly felt that she wanted to get out of that room more than anything. It felt as if something was coming; as if, in another moment or two, something would solidify out of sunlight. She ran for the door to the stairs and clattered down them, making a tremendous noise.

Even in the parlour that twitching between her shoulders was still with her, and made her walk backwards almost all the way to the door into the hall. And once she was out in the

hall, she had to look behind her again
– she had to glance up at the spy-hole
that looked through the wall of the
big bedroom and down into the hall.
There it was, the square hole. She
kept her eyes on it as she backed
across the expanse of the hall floor.
And she saw the shadows up there
move. Something in the frame of the
spy-hole moved.

She stopped and stared, feeling her
heart begin to race again. Shadows
were moving across the walls of the
big bedroom and she could glimpse
them through the spy-hole, that was
all. But as she turned her head away,
she saw – a smile. Whatever she saw,
she saw it too briefly to say it was a
face; and certainly too briefly to say it
was a man's face, or a woman's face, or
any other sort of face. All she saw was
shadow-movement; but the shadows
moved in a smile.

She turned and ran as hard as she
could across the hall, across the passage and into the kitchen.

'Hold up!' Mr Wheeler said. 'What are you? A racehorse?'

'Your dinner's getting cold,' her mother said.

It was while Michaela was tackling her portion of apple crumble and custard that her tooth came out, quite painlessly. She took it out of her mouth and held it up for her mother and Mr Wheeler to see, and then placed it beside her plate. 'The tooth fairy'll give me ten pence for that, won't she?' She was glad to have something safe and ordinary to talk about, like tooth fairies.

'If Jack'll let the tooth fairy in,' Mrs Lloyd said. 'If we're allowed to go to bed tonight.'

Michaela slid down from her chair, went over to where the broken pieces of dish were still lying on the floor, and began picking them up.

'Be careful you don't cut yourself,' Mrs Lloyd said, and kept a wary eye on the dresser where the other dishes were stacked, while she cleared the table off.

But even when Michaela had fetched the dustpan and brush and had swept up the littlest broken bits, no other dish had been thrown down. 'I think Jack'll let the tooth fairy in,' she said.

'He's just on his best behaviour because Mr Wheeler's here,' her mother said.

Mr Wheeler was peering at Michaela's tooth, which was still lying on the table. 'I should think the tooth fairy'll give you fifty pence for a beautiful tooth like that,' he said. 'Fifty pence for sure.'

CHAPTER SEVEN

Michaela came up from another night's deep blankness to find the world still there: the sun shining, the traffic passing by on the road outside, and the sounds of her mother washing in the bathroom.

She lay wondering what there was to remember for that day, and what she would have for breakfast, and what she would do later . . . She had slept well and deeply. Jack hadn't disturbed them again. He must have accepted her apology— Well, hadn't he smiled at her?

Then she remembered her tooth.

She sat up in bed, lifted the pillow –
and stared.

She had known there would be
a silver ten pence piece under the
pillow. She'd hoped there might be a
fifty pence piece. But she'd never
expected the coin that she saw.

She could tell it was old, just by
looking at it. It was dirty, as much
black as it was silver, and it wasn't a
perfect circle. It was squashed in at
the sides. She picked it up, expecting
to find it warm to touch, as the
tuning-pipes always were when Jack

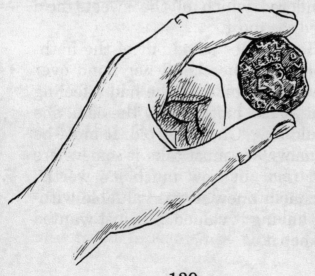

had been playing with them. But the coin was cool to her fingers.

One side had some clumsy writing around the edge, which she couldn't read, and a cross. The other side had a funny man's face with a crown on top – it was more like a drawing that she might do herself than anything on a modern coin.

She knew it hadn't come from any tooth fairy. She knew it was from Jack. What would Jack want with her old tooth? The coin was to show that they were friends again. She wondered which of the sweets he'd liked the most.

Her mother came out of the bathroom, and she closed her hand over the coin, to hide it. She had a feeling that, if her mother saw the coin, she would say, 'Oh, that's old. It must be valuable. We must take it somewhere and find out how much it's worth.' Michaela knew it was valuable without having it valued. She just wanted to keep it.

'The tooth fairy been?' her mother asked. Michaela nodded. 'Toast and cereal for breakfast? Hurry up and get washed and dressed and I'll put the toast on.'

When Michaela went downstairs into the kitchen, the old coin was hidden in her pocket. A ripple of welcoming knocks around the walls welcomed her.

'Go on, knock,' Mrs Lloyd said. 'Give us another performance like the other night's and you get no more porridge out of me.'

Michaela had her hand in her pocket, feeling the worn smoothness of the old coin. She said nothing of why Jack had thrown invisible wardrobes about and chased them from the house. She didn't think her mother would want to hear it.

Nearly a week later, Michaela still hadn't said anything to her mother, or shown her the coin. She didn't think she ever would. The whole matter was between her and Jack. But when Mr Wheeler came to see them again, she told him. She thought that he ought to know.

They were sitting in the parlour while Mrs Lloyd was in the kitchen, making tea and sandwiches. 'You know the boy who played the trick on Jack a long time ago?' Michaela began.

Mr Wheeler nodded.

'You know how the man who used to live here made it up to Jack that time by giving him beer?'

Mr Wheeler nodded again.

'Well, I gave him sweets,' Michaela said. 'And my tuning-pipes. And he hasn't frightened us since.'

'Good,' Mr Wheeler said.

'And he left me this – under my pillow,' Michaela said and, after a quick glance to make sure her mother wasn't coming, she took the coin from her pocket and put it into Mr Wheeler's hand.

Mr Wheeler let it lie on his hand for a moment, then peered at it. 'Now, that's old,' he said. He looked up at her. 'That's lucky. Even when my grandson comes back and you have to leave here, you'll always have this.'

From the empty air between their heads and the ceiling fell a shower of music, a short, delicate snatch of tune. For a moment after it ended, they both stayed with their heads raised, waiting for more.

'That's Jack,' Michaela said, when Mr Wheeler still stared. 'I'm glad I gave him the pipes. He can play tunes on them. I never could. There were too many and I could never blow them fast enough.'

Mrs Lloyd shouldered the parlour door open then, with a tray of sandwiches. Knock, knock, knock went Jack on the wall above the door. Michaela quickly took the coin back from Mr Wheeler and put it into her pocket. Her hand touched something else, something papery, and she pulled it out.

It was a paper bag of cherry kisses!

THE END